D0842523

YASMIN

The Explorer

WITHDRAWN

written by
SAADIA FARUQI

illustrated by
HATEM ALY

PICTURE WINDOW BOOKS
a capstone imprint

To Mariam for inspiring me, and
Mubashir for helping me find the
right words —S.F.

To my sister, Eman, and her amazing
girls, Jana and Kenzi —H.A.

Yasmin is published by Picture Window Books,
a Capstone Imprint
1710 Roe Crest Drive
North Mankato, Minnesota 56003
www.mycapstone.com

Text © 2019 Saadia Faruqi
Illustrations © 2019 Picture Window Books

Cataloging-in-Publication Data is available on the Library of
Congress website.

ISBN: 978-1-5158-2729-0 (hardcover)
978-1-5158-2732-0 (paperback)
978-1-5158-2736-8 (ebook pdf)

Summary: Every explorer needs a map! Baba encourages Yasmin
to make one of her own. But when Yasmin loses sight of Mama at
the farmer's market, can her map bring them back together?

Editor: Kristen Mohn
Designer: Aruna Rangarajan

Design Elements:
Shutterstock: Art and Fashion, rangsan paidaen

Printed and bound in the United States of America.
PA021

TABLE OF CONTENTS

CHAPTER 1

Ancient Maps

One afternoon Yasmin sat reading with Baba.

"A long time ago, explorers used big paper maps to find their way," Baba said.

"What's an explorer?" asked Yasmin.

"Someone who discovers new places. An adventurer," Baba said.

Yasmin looked at the maps in Baba's book. There were straight roads and curvy roads. There were lakes and rivers and forests.

"I want to be an explorer!" she said.

"Well, then, the first thing you'll need is a map," Baba replied.

Yasmin clapped her hands.

"I'll make a map of our

neighborhood."

"Good idea," Baba said.

Yasmin found crayons and

paper.

She drew their house. Down the street was the market. Near that was the park.

"This is excellent, jaan!" Baba said, using his sweet name for her.

Soon Mama came in.

"Yasmin, I'm going to the farmer's market. Want to come with me?"

Yasmin jumped up. "Yes! It will be an exploration!" She could hardly wait as Mama got her hijab and purse.

"Don't forget your map!" Baba said. "Every explorer needs a map."

⋟ CHAPTER 2 ⋞

The Farmer's Market

Mama and Yasmin walked down the street to the farmer's market. The air was fresh and smelled like flowers.

"This way to the market, Mama!" Yasmin said, pointing at her map.

The street
was crowded.
There were people
everywhere!

"Hold my hand,
Yasmin. I don't want
you to get lost,"
Mama warned.

Their first
stop was the fruit
seller. Mama bought
strawberries and
bananas.

Yasmin sat down on the sidewalk and added the fruit seller to her map.

Their next stop was the bakery stall. It had all sorts of breads, and they all smelled delicious!

Thin ones and fat ones. Big ones and small ones. Yum!

"Two naan, please!" Mama called out.

Yasmin added the bakery stall to her map.

There were so many good smells and things to see. Yasmin saw a man holding balloons. Down the street a lady was selling roses. An ice-cream truck was parked at the corner. Finally, she found what she was looking for. The playground! Yasmin was itching to explore.

"Mama, the park! I'll be right back!"

CHAPTER 3

A Map to the Rescue

Yasmin ran over to the swings. Swings were her favorite!

Up, up, up!

Then she headed to the sandbox. She would dig for buried treasure!

Yasmin was having so much
fun pretending. Then she thought
of something. Where was Mama?

Yasmin looked around, but
there were too many kids.

Uh-oh.

Yasmin took a deep breath.
"I'm a brave explorer,"
she reminded
herself. "I can
find my way
back to Mama."

She still
had her map.
She unrolled it
and studied it.

She looked toward the man

with the balloons. Then the lady

selling roses, and the ice-cream

truck. She saw the fruit seller

where Mama bought

strawberries. And she saw

the bakery stall where Mama

bought the naan.

But no Mama.

Yasmin told herself not to cry.

Explorers don't cry.

Then she saw Mama's blue hijab. She ran toward her. "Mama!"

"There you are, Yasmin!" Mama said. "I was looking for you! You must tell me where you're going!"

"I did, but you didn't hear me. I'm sorry," Yasmin said, crying in relief.

"Let's go home and make dinner," Mama said and hugged Yasmin close. "Baba will be waiting for us."

Yasmin nodded. Next time she
went exploring, she would take her
map *and* Mama!

Think About It, Talk About It

* Getting lost can be very scary. Think about what you would do if you got lost. Talk with your family and come up with a plan.

* If you could explore anywhere in the world, where would you go? What supplies would you take along?

* Think about your neighborhood. Are there houses and apartments? Is there a park or a school or a store nearby? Draw a map and show it to your family.

Learn Urdu with Yasmin!

Yasmin's family speaks both English and Urdu. Urdu is a language from Pakistan. Maybe you already know some Urdu words!

baba (BAH-bah)—father

hijab (HEE-jahb)—scarf covering the hair

jaan (jahn)—life; a sweet nickname for a loved one

kameez (kuh-MEEZ)—long tunic or shirt

mama (MAH-mah)—mother

naan (nahn)—flatbread baked in the oven

nana (NAH-nah)—grandfather on mother's side

nani (NAH-nee)—grandmother on mother's side

sari (SAHR-ee)—dress worn by women in South Asia

Pakistan Facts

Yasmin and her family are proud of their Pakistani culture. Yasmin loves to share facts about Pakistan!

Islamabad

PAKISTAN

Location

Pakistan is on the continent of Asia, with India on one side and Afghanistan on the other.

Currency

The currency, or money, of Pakistan is called the rupee.

Language

The national language of Pakistan is Urdu, but English and several other languages are also spoken there.

سلام

(Salaam means Peace)

History

Independence Day in Pakistan is celebrated on August 14.

A Taste of Pakistan

Mango Lassi (Yogurt Drink)

Ingredients:
- a few ice cubes
- 1 cup (240 ml) plain yogurt
- ½ cup (120 ml) water
- 2 teaspoons (8 g) sugar
- ½ cup (120 ml) canned mango pulp

Directions:
Crush the ice cubes in a blender. Add yogurt, water, sugar, and mango. Blend for about one minute. Serve cold.

Try this! If you don't have canned mango, other crushed fruit is yummy too. Try peach or banana!

Saadia Faruqi is a Pakistani American writer, interfaith activist, and cultural sensitivity trainer previously profiled in *O Magazine*. She is author of the adult short-story collection, *Brick Walls: Tales of Hope & Courage from Pakistan*. Her essays have been published in *Huffington Post*, *Upworthy*, and *NBC Asian America*. She resides in Houston, Texas, with her husband and children.

Hatem Aly is an Egyptian-born illustrator whose work has been featured in multiple publications worldwide. He currently lives in beautiful New Brunswick, Canada, with his wife, son, and more pets than people. When he is not dipping cookies in a cup of tea or staring at blank pieces of paper, he is usually drawing books. One of the books he illustrated is *The Inquisitor's Tale* by Adam Gidwitz, which won a Newbery Honor and other awards, despite Hatem's drawings of a farting dragon, a two-headed cat, and stinky cheese.

Join Yasmin on all her adventures!

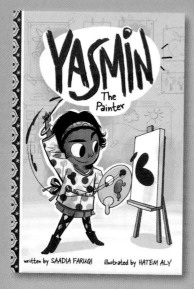

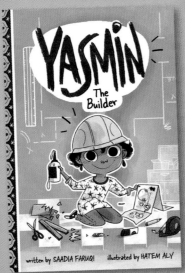
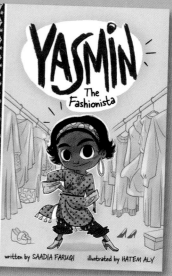

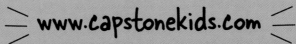

31901063985164